C'MERE, BOY!

For puppy Hobbes and Guy DiLena — S.J.

To Rod, Gloria and Shane for their love, support and so much laughter — A.S.

Text © 2010 Sharon Jennings
Illustrations © 2010 Ashley Spires

Kids Can Press acknowledges the financial support of the Government of Ontario, through the Ontario Media Development Corporation's Ontario Book Initiative; the Ontario Arts Council; the Canada Council for the Arts; and the Government of Canada, through the BPIDP, for our publishing activity.

Published in Canada by
Kids Can Press Ltd.
29 Birch Avenue
Toronto, ON M4V 1E2

Published in the U.S. by
Kids Can Press Ltd.
2250 Military Road
Tonawanda, NY 14150

www.kidscanpress.com

Kids Can Press is a Corus™ Entertainment company

The artwork in this book was rendered in ink, watercolor, digital collage and sheer determination.
The text is set in Big Ruckus AOE.

Edited by Tara Walker
Designed by Karen Powers
Printed and bound in China

This book is smyth sewn casebound.

CM 10 0 9 8 7 6 5 4 3 2 1

LIBRARY AND ARCHIVES CANADA CATALOGUING IN PUBLICATION

Jennings, Sharon
    C'mere, boy! / written by Sharon Jennings ; illustrated by Ashley Spires.

ISBN 978-1-55453-440-1 (bound)

1. Dogs—Juvenile fiction. I. Spires, Ashley, 1978— II. Title.

PS8569.E563C64 2010   jC813'.54   C2009-903626-6

C'MERE, BOY!

Written by Sharon Jennings

Illustrated by Ashley Spires

KIDS CAN PRESS

og wanted a boy. He asked his mama,
"Can we get a boy? Can we? Please? Can we?"

Dog's mama looked around the doghouse and
said, "We don't have room for a boy. And who
would take care of him?"

Dog answered, "He can sleep in my bed.
And I'll take care of him. I'll play with him, and
I'll take him for walks. I promise."

Mama smiled. "It's up to you," she said.
"But remember, a boy is hard to train."

On Monday, Dog wrote "BOY FOOD" on the grocery list.

His mama scratched it off. "You don't have a boy yet," she said.

"I know," answered Dog. "But when I have a boy, I can feed him."

On Tuesday, Dog came home with a leash. His mama laughed. "You don't have a boy yet," she said.

"I know," answered Dog. "But when I have a boy, I can walk him."

On Wednesday, Dog went to the obedience school. A sign read,

LEARN NEW TRICKS!

"Why are you here?" asked the teacher. "You don't have a boy."

"I know," answered Dog. "But when I have a boy, I can teach him."

On Thursday, Dog went to The Posh Pooch Spa for a haircut and pedicure.

"How are you going to pay?" asked the owner. "You don't have a boy."

"I know," agreed Dog. "But when I have a boy, I want to look good."

"Out!" said the owner.

"Phooey!" said Dog. "I can't do anything until I get a boy."

On Friday, Dog told his mama he was going shopping.

"I'm not coming home until I find a boy," he said.

irst, he went to the mall. A sign read,

NO DOGS ALLOWED!

Dog was ordered off the premises.

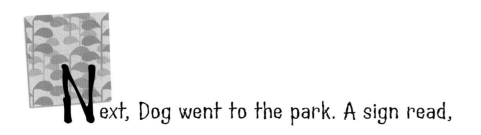 ext, Dog went to the park. A sign read,

DOGS MUST BE ON A LEASH

Dog was chased away.

And so, Dog walked up and down the streets. He saw lots of boys. Some boys were too big. Some boys were too small. But most importantly, none of the boys smelled just right.

Soon, it was too dark to see anything. So Dog did not see the big van driving along behind him with a sign that read,

DOG CATCHER

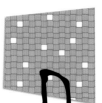og was put into a kennel. A man gave him food and water. Dog did not sleep very well. He missed his mama. "Maybe..." thought Dog, "maybe I should forget about getting a boy."

On Saturday, Dog was taken out to the meet 'n' greet room. A boy was waiting.

"C'mere, boy," said the boy.

Dog was confused. "No, you c'mere, Boy," he answered.

Boy did as he was told. He walked over to Dog and scratched his ears.

Dog nuzzled Boy's hand.

Dog sniffed Boy's bum.

Dog licked Boy's face.

"You are the right boy!" announced Dog. "I'll take you!"

Dog and Boy did not go back to Dog's house. Instead, they rode in a car to Boy's house.

"Now, you said you'd take care of him," Boy's mama warned.

"I will," said Boy. "I promise."

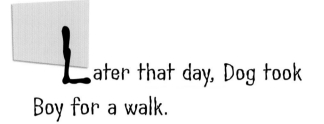 ater that day, Dog took Boy for a walk.

Dog taught Boy how to play fetch.

Dog taught Boy how to stoop and scoop.

And at suppertime, Dog taught Boy how to share his food.

On Sunday, Dog wrote a letter.

Dear Mama,

I finally got a boy! You were right. Training him isn't easy. But I'm going to keep him, and I will live in his house for now. Will visit you soon.

Love,
Dog